In this, his first collection of tales for young readers, John Gardner's stunning and irreverent pen brings to the fairy tale a slyly humorous, contemporary flare. Here, as in the classic tales, princes, witches, dragons and giants play their age-old mysterious games against a background of magic forests and haunted castles. Yet all the mysteries, however ancient, are made new in this surprising new addition to a timeless tradition.

DRAGON, DRAGON
and Other Tales

JOHN GARDNER

DRAGON, DRAGON
and Other Tales

Illustrated by Charles Shields

ALFRED A. KNOPF NEW YORK

THIS IS A BORZOI BOOK PUBLISHED BY ALFRED A. KNOPF, INC.

Text Copyright © 1975 by Boskydell Artists Ltd. Illustrations Copyright © 1975 by Charles Shields. All rights reserved under International and Pan-American Copyright Conventions. Published in the United States by Alfred A. Knopf, Inc., New York, and simultaneously in Canada by Random House of Canada Limited, Toronto. Distributed by Random House, Inc., New York. Library of Congress Cataloging in Publication Data. Gardner, John Champlin, 1933–Dragon, dragon, and other tales

SUMMARY

Four fairy tales featuring a dragon, a giant, a cunning mule, and a little chimney-girl. 1. Fairy tales. [1. Fairy tales] I. Shields, Charles. II. Title. pz8.G216Dr [398.2] 75-2542. ISBN 0-394-83122-5. ISBN 0-394-93122-X lib. bdg. Manufactured in the United States of America 098765432

To Joel and Lucy

Contents

DRAGON, DRAGON

There was once a king whose kingdom was plagued by a dragon. The king did not know which way to turn. The king's knights were all cowards who hid under their beds whenever the dragon came in sight, so they were of no use to the king at all. And the king's wizard could not help either because, being old, he had forgotten his magic spells. Nor could the wizard look up the spells that had slipped his mind, for he had unfortunately misplaced his wizard's book many years before. The king was at his wit's end.

Every time there was a full moon the dragon came out of his lair and ravaged the countryside. He frightened maidens and stopped up chimneys and broke store windows and set people's clocks back and made dogs bark until no one could hear himself think.

He tipped over fences and robbed graves and put frogs in people's drinking water and tore the last chapters out of novels and changed house numbers around so that people crawled into bed with their neighbors' wives.

He stole spark plugs out of people's cars and put

firecrackers in people's cigars and stole the clappers from all the church bells and sprung every bear trap for miles around so the bears could wander wherever they pleased.

And to top it all off, he changed around all the roads in the kingdom so that people could not get anywhere except by starting out in the wrong direction.

"That," said the king in a fury, "is enough!" And he called a meeting of everyone in the kingdom.

Now it happened that there lived in the kingdom a wise old cobbler who had a wife and three sons. The cobbler and his family came to the king's meeting and stood way in back by the door, for the cobbler had a feeling that since he was nobody important there had probably been some mistake, and no doubt the king had intended the meeting for everyone in the kingdom except his family and him.

"Ladies and gentlemen," said the king when everyone was present, "I've put up with that dragon as long as I can. He has got to be stopped."

All the people whispered amongst themselves, and the king smiled, pleased with the impression he had made.

But the wise cobbler said gloomily, "It's all very well to talk about it—but how are you going to do it?"

And now all the people smiled and winked as if to say, "Well, King, he's got you there!"

The king frowned.

"It's not that His Majesty hasn't tried," the queen spoke up loyally.

"Yes," said the king, "I've told my knights again and again that they ought to slay that dragon. But I can't *force* them to go. I'm not a tyrant."

"Why doesn't the wizard say a magic spell?" asked the cobbler.

"He's done the best he can," said the king.

The wizard blushed and everyone looked embarrassed. "I used to do all sorts of spells and chants when I was younger," the wizard explained. "But I've lost my spell book, and I begin to fear I'm losing my memory too. For instance, I've been trying for days to recall one spell I used to do. I forget, just now, what the deuce it was for. It went something like—

> *Bimble,*
> *Wimble,*
> *Cha, Cha*
> CHOOMPF!

Suddenly, to everyone's surprise, the queen turned into a rosebush.

"Oh dear," said the wizard.

"Now you've done it," groaned the king.

"Poor Mother," said the princess.

"I don't know what can have happened," the wizard

said nervously, "but don't worry, I'll have her changed back in a jiffy." He shut his eyes and racked his brain for a spell that would change her back.

But the king said quickly, "You'd better leave well enough alone. If you change her into a rattlesnake we'll have to chop off her head."

Meanwhile the cobbler stood with his hands in his pockets, sighing at the waste of time. "About the dragon . . ." he began.

"Oh yes," said the king. "I'll tell you what I'll do. I'll give the princess' hand in marriage to anyone who can make the dragon stop."

"It's not enough," said the cobbler. "She's a nice enough girl, you understand. But how would an ordinary person support her? Also, what about those of us that are already married?"

"In that case," said the king, "I'll offer the princess' hand or half the kingdom or both—whichever is most convenient."

The cobbler scratched his chin and considered it. "It's not enough," he said at last. "It's a good enough kingdom, you understand, but it's too much responsibility."

"Take it or leave it," the king said.

"I'll leave it," said the cobbler. And he shrugged and went home.

But the cobbler's eldest son thought the bargain was

a good one, for the princess was very beautiful and he liked the idea of having half the kingdom to run as he pleased. So he said to the king, "I'll accept those terms, Your Majesty. By tomorrow morning the dragon will be slain."

"Bless you!" cried the king.

"Hooray, hooray, hooray!" cried all the people, throwing their hats in the air.

The cobbler's eldest son beamed with pride, and the second eldest looked at him enviously. The youngest son said timidly, "Excuse me, Your Majesty, but don't you think the queen looks a little unwell? If I were you I think I'd water her."

"Good heavens," cried the king, glancing at the queen who had been changed into a rosebush, "I'm glad you mentioned it!"

Now the cobbler's eldest son was very clever and was known far and wide for how quickly he could multiply fractions in his head. He was perfectly sure he could slay the dragon by somehow or other playing a trick on him, and he didn't feel that he needed his wise old father's advice. But he thought it was only polite to ask, and so he went to his father, who was working as usual at his cobbler's bench, and said, "Well, Father, I'm off to slay the dragon. Have you any advice to give me?"

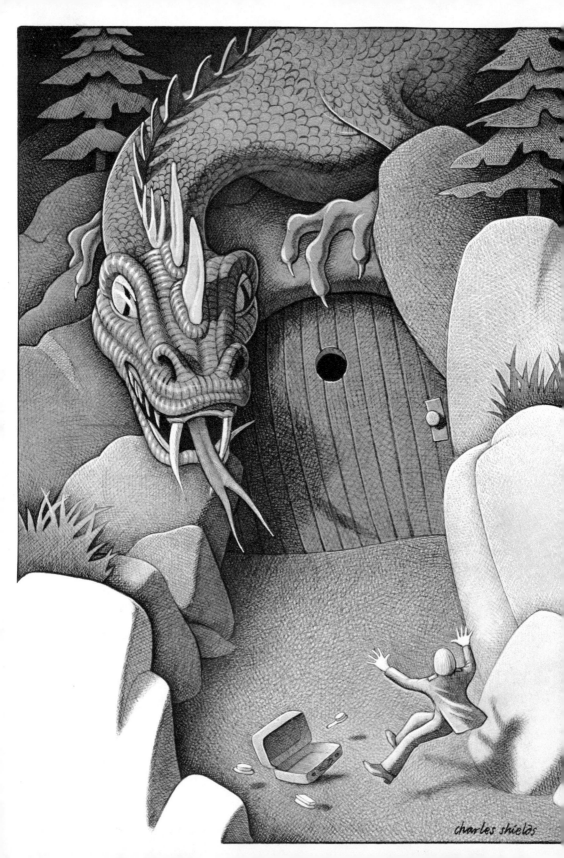

charles shields

The cobbler thought a moment and replied, "When and if you come to the dragon's lair, recite the following poem.

> *Dragon, dragon, how do you do?*
> *I've come from the king to murder you.*

Say it very loudly and firmly and the dragon will fall, God willing, at your feet."

"How curious!" said the eldest son. And he thought to himself, "The old man is not as wise as I thought. If I say something like that to the dragon, he will eat me up in an instant. The way to kill a dragon is to out-fox him." And keeping his opinion to himself, the eldest son set forth on his quest.

When he came at last to the dragon's lair, which was a cave, the eldest son slyly disguised himself as a peddler and knocked on the door and called out, "Hello there!"

"There's nobody home!" roared a voice.

The voice was as loud as an earthquake, and the eldest son's knees knocked together in terror.

"I don't come to trouble you," the eldest son said meekly. "I merely thought you might be interested in looking at some of our brushes. Or if you'd prefer," he added quickly, "I could leave our catalogue with you and I could drop by again, say, early next week."

"I don't want any brushes," the voice roared, "and I especially don't want any brushes next week."

"Oh," said the eldest son. By now his knees were knocking together so badly that he had to sit down.

Suddenly a great shadow fell over him, and the eldest son looked up. It was the dragon. The eldest son drew his sword, but the dragon lunged and swallowed him in a single gulp, sword and all, and the eldest son found himself in the dark of the dragon's belly. "What a fool I was not to listen to my wise old father!" thought the eldest son. And he began to weep bitterly.

"Well," sighed the king the next morning, "I see the dragon has not been slain yet."

"I'm just as glad, personally," said the princess, sprinkling the queen. "I would have had to marry that eldest son, and he had warts."

Now the cobbler's middle son decided it was his turn to try. The middle son was very strong and was known far and wide for being able to lift up the corner of a church. He felt perfectly sure he could slay the dragon by simply laying into him, but he thought it would be only polite to ask his father's advice. So he went to his father and said to him, "Well, Father, I'm off to slay the dragon. Have you any advice for me?"

The cobbler told the middle son exactly what he'd told the eldest.

"When and if you come to the dragon's lair, recite the following poem.

> *Dragon, dragon, how do you do?*
> *I've come from the king to murder you.*

Say it very loudly and firmly, and the dragon will fall, God willing, at your feet."

"What an odd thing to say," thought the middle son. "The old man is not as wise as I thought. You have to take these dragons by surprise." But he kept his opinion to himself and set forth.

When he came in sight of the dragon's lair, the middle son spurred his horse to a gallop and thundered into the entrance swinging his sword with all his might.

But the dragon had seen him while he was still a long way off, and being very clever, the dragon had crawled up on top of the door so that when the son came charging in he went under the dragon and on to the back of the cave and slammed into the wall. Then the dragon chuckled and got down off the door, taking his time, and strolled back to where the man and the horse lay unconscious from the terrific blow. Opening his mouth as if for a yawn, the dragon swallowed the middle son in a single gulp and put the horse in the freezer to eat another day.

"What a fool I was not to listen to my wise old

father," thought the middle son when he came to in the dragon's belly. And he too began to weep bitterly.

That night there was a full moon, and the dragon ravaged the countryside so terribly that several families moved to another kingdom.

"Well," sighed the king in the morning, "still no luck in this dragon business, I see."

"I'm just as glad, myself," said the princess, moving her mother, pot and all, to the window where the sun could get at her. "The cobbler's middle son was a kind of humpback."

Now the cobbler's youngest son saw that his turn had come. He was very upset and nervous, and he wished he had never been born. He was not clever, like his eldest brother, and he was not strong, like his second-eldest brother. He was a decent, honest boy who always minded his elders.

He borrowed a suit of armor from a friend of his who was a knight, and when the youngest son put the armor on it was so heavy he could hardly walk. From another knight he borrowed a sword, and that was so heavy that the only way the youngest son could get it to the dragon's lair was to drag it along behind his horse like a plow.

When everything was in readiness, the youngest son went for a last conversation with his father.

12

"Father, have you any advice to give me?" he asked.

"Only this," said the cobbler. "When and if you come to the dragon's lair, recite the following poem.

> *Dragon, dragon, how do you do?*
> *I've come from the king to murder you.*

Say it very loudly and firmly, and the dragon will fall, God willing, at your feet."

"Are you certain?" asked the youngest son uneasily.

"As certain as one can ever be in these matters," said the wise old cobbler.

And so the youngest son set forth on his quest. He traveled over hill and dale and at last came to the dragon's cave.

The dragon, who had seen the cobbler's youngest son while he was still a long way off, was seated up above the door, inside the cave, waiting and smiling to himself. But minutes passed and no one came thundering in. The dragon frowned, puzzled, and was tempted to peek out. However, reflecting that patience seldom goes unrewarded, the dragon kept his head up out of sight and went on waiting. At last, when he could stand it no longer, the dragon craned his neck and looked. There at the entrance of the cave stood a trembling young man in a suit of armor twice his size, struggling with a sword so heavy he could lift only one end of it at a time.

charles shields

At sight of the dragon, the cobbler's youngest -
began to tremble so violently that his armor r
a house caving in. He heaved with all h˙
sword and got the handle up level w˙
even now the point was down in the a..
and firmly as he could manage, the young‿
cried—

> *Dragon, dragon, how do you do?*
> *I've come from the king to murder you!*

"What?" cried the dragon, flabbergasted. "You? *You?*
Murder *Me???*" All at once he began to laugh, pointing
at the little cobbler's son. *"He he he ho ha!"* he roared,
shaking all over, and tears filled his eyes. *"He he he ho
ho ho ha ha!"* laughed the dragon. He was laughing so
hard he had to hang onto his sides, and he fell off the
door and landed on his back, still laughing, kicking his
legs helplessly, rolling from side to side, laughing and
laughing and laughing.

The cobbler's son was annoyed. "I *do* come from the
king to murder you," he said. "A person doesn't like to
be laughed at for a thing like that."

"He he he!" wailed the dragon, almost sobbing, gasp-
ing for breath. "Of course not, poor dear boy! But
really, *he he*, the *idea* of it, *ha ha ha!* And that simply
ridiculous *poem!"* Tears streamed from the dragon's
eyes and he lay on his back perfectly helpless with
laughter.

15

"It's a good poem," said the cobbler's youngest son loyally. "My father made it up." And growing angrier he shouted, "I want you to stop that laughing, or I'll —I'll—" But the dragon could not stop for the life of him. And suddenly, in a terrific rage, the cobbler's son began flopping the sword end over end in the direction of the dragon. Sweat ran off the youngest son's forehead, but he labored on, blistering mad, and at last, with one supreme heave, he had the sword standing on its handle a foot from the dragon's throat. Of its own weight the sword fell, slicing the dragon's head off.

"He he ho huk," went the dragon—and then he lay dead.

The two older brothers crawled out and thanked their younger brother for saving their lives. "We have learned our lesson," they said.

Then the three brothers gathered all the treasures from the dragon's cave and tied them to the back end of the youngest brother's horse, and tied the dragon's head on behind the treasures, and started home. "I'm glad I listened to my father," the youngest son thought. "Now I'll be the richest man in the kingdom."

There were hand-carved picture frames and silver spoons and boxes of jewels and chests of money and silver compasses and maps telling where there were more treasures buried when these ran out. There was also a curious old book with a picture of an owl on the

cover, and inside, poems and odd sentences and rec-
ipes that seemed to make no sense.

When they reached the king's castle the people all
leaped for joy to see that the dragon was dead, and the
princess ran out and kissed the youngest brother on
the forehead, for secretly she had hoped it would be
him.

"Well," said the king, "which half of the kingdom
do you want?"

"My wizard's book!" exclaimed the wizard. "He's
found my wizard's book!" He opened the book and
ran his finger along under the words and then said in a
loud voice, "Glmuzk, shkzmlp, blam!"

Instantly the queen stood before them in her natural
shape, except she was soaking wet from being sprin-
kled too often. She glared at the king.

"Oh dear," said the king, hurrying toward the door.

THE TAILOR
AND THE GIANT

Once there was a kingdom where everything was perfect except for one thing. On the first Monday of every month a giant would come and eat everything he could catch. First he ate up all the horses, then he ate up all the cows, then he ate up the ministers, and then he began on the schoolteachers. People began to be worried because, though it wasn't so bad about the horses or cows or ministers or schoolteachers, what might the giant think of next? The king said, "Something has got to be done," and he made a law that every man in the kingdom had to take a course in self-defense and serve for thirty days in the royal army so that the realm would be adequately protected at all times.

Now in this kingdom there lived a timid little tailor. He was so timid that sometimes he wouldn't walk home from his shop for months at a stretch, for fear that on the way a dog might bite him, or he might be beaten up by a band of young cutthroats, or a flowerpot might fall on his head from a second-story window. When he read in the paper that every man in the kingdom was going to have to serve in the royal army, he began to shake like a leaf.

"I won't do it!" he thought. "I'll paint a sign and I'll demonstrate in front of the palace." Immediately he began making signs which said LOVE in big red letters. But when the signs were finished and the tailor had put on his coat and mittens and stocking cap, he realized he was afraid to leave his shop. He was afraid of more than mere dogs or young cutthroats or flowerpots now. He was afraid his neighbors might laugh at him, or that the king might be cross, or that the signs might incidentally call the giant's attention to him and thus get him eaten. Furthermore, as he said to himself, what if he should turn his ankle on the cobblestones in front of the palace and end up horribly crippled and out of work? And so he sat down in the middle of his shop to think.

It was there, on the first Monday of the month, that the giant found him.

"Ar *har!*" said the giant. "What have we here? I do believe it's nothing else but a fat little tailor!"

The giant was so big that to look into the tailor shop he had to kneel down in the street and press his cheek against the pavement. All the tailor could see of him was his enormous, watery eye, and the tailor was so terrified he couldn't so much as squeak.

charles shields

The giant said, "What luck! I was saying to Moranda just this morning,

> *Moranda, Moranda, get ready for meat!*
> *Today I will bring you a Tailor to eat!*

At that, the tailor shook worse than ever and thought surely he would die of fright.

But just that moment a cheer went up from the people who were watching, for who should be coming down the tailor's street but the king himself and the royal thirty-day army. When His Majesty saw the giant he hastily ducked down an alley, yelling, "Charge, brave boys!" And they charged, being mostly young and foolish. Before the giant knew what was happening, the gallant little army of tinkers and watchmakers and plowboys and bank clerks had scratched up his face with their keen-edged weapons till he looked like he'd just come running through a prickler patch.

The giant was furious, and howling with rage, he snatched up the whole gallant army in his two hands and went thundering home, bellowing unto the heavens as he went,

> *Moranda, Moranda, get ready for meat!*
> *Today I will bring you an Army to eat!*

The timid little tailor, who had seen it all, was so

moved by the courage of the gallant little army that he could scarcely contain himself. "Oh why can't *I* be brave like that?" he cried out, wringing his fingers. However, he wasn't the type, and he knew it, and there was an end of it. And so he sat in the middle of the shop, sunk deep in gloom, and wished he had never been born.

The king, meanwhile, was extremely annoyed at having lost all his army at one fell swoop, and he made a law that from now on every man in the kingdom would have to serve for *ninety* days in the royal army so that the realm would be adequately protected at all times. He put his new law in all the papers and sent it through the realm by messengers and had copies of it nailed to every lamppost in every town from one border to the other, and before long the law came to the lamppost in front of the tailor shop.

The tailor, squinting cautiously past the curtain on his front window, read the royal proclamation and shook to his boots and thought, "I won't do it. How can I? How can they ask it?" However, he did not feel righteous about not doing it this time, for he remembered those gallant young tinkers and watchmakers and plowboys and bank clerks who had saved his life before. And soon it occurred to him that probably *no* one would want to be a member of the army now, having seen what could happen to a brave little army.

Immediately the tailor was indignant, as a citizen, and he realized what his duty was. He began making signs which said JOIN NOW! in big red letters, and he nailed them to sticks for carrying, and when he was finished he intended to march in front of the palace and rouse up the nation. But when the signs were finished the thought of young cutthroats and dogs and falling flowerpots came flitting through his mind, and then, worse, the thought that the people might be irritated at his seeming to be holier-than-thou, and the king might be insulted, and the giant might tend to especially notice a person carrying a sign. So he sat in the middle of his shop and trembled and grieved and tried to think.

It was another first Monday of the month, as it happened. Before long, along came the giant, and he got down on his knees and looked into the tailor shop and there sat the timid little tailor, grieving and shaking.

"Ar *har!*" said the giant. "As you see, I'm back. I was saying to Moranda just this morning,

Moranda, Moranda, get ready for meat!
Today I will bring you a Tailor to eat!

And sure enough, he opened the front door of the tailor shop with the tips of two fingers and began to reach in for the tailor.

But just that moment a great cheer went up from the people standing by, for who should come marching down the street but His Majesty the King and his royal ninety-day army. The ninety-day army was somewhat smaller than the thirty-day army, but it was even more gallant, being even younger and less experienced. The king ducked hastily into an alley and yelled, "Charge, brave boys!" and they charged. Before the giant knew what was happening he was scratched and slivered to an inch of his life and one of his eyes was swollen shut.

The giant was furious, and bellowing with rage he seized the army in his two hands and went hurrying home, yelling as he went,

> *Moranda, Moranda, get ready for meat!*
> *Today I will bring you an Army to eat!*

The timid little tailor, who had not made a sound in all this time, unable to bring out so much as a squeak, now managed a feeble little "Hooray!"—for he was moved to the depths of his soul by the army's gallantry. Also, he devoutly wished that he'd never been born.

"Woe is me," said the tailor, sunk in gloom, sitting wringing his fingers in the middle of the shop, "I don't deserve to live, and that's the truth." After a moment he frowned and said, "That really *is* true, you know? I really *don't* deserve to live!" The vague idea of jumping off a bridge occurred to him, and he was so frightened by this turn of thought that he began to whistle, trying to cheer himself up. But the thought came again, persistent. "A person as cowardly as you, little tailor, really and truly does not deserve to live." He shuddered.

Darkness had by now fallen, and as often happened when darkness fell, the tall, narrow buildings on the tailor's street looked higher than usual, obscurely dangerous with their crooked chimneys and eye-like, gaping windows. The alleys, where the dogs ran, hunting through garbage or chasing rats or biting passers-by, and the subterranean rooms and ditches where bands of young cutthroats held their meetings and said their secret passwords and burned their secret candles, all were more frightening than usual now. The weight of night lay over the city like giant crows' wings, and even the king's daughter the princess, sitting propped in pillows in her wide, warm bed, surrounded by all her ladies-in-waiting, felt queasy.

The poor miserable little tailor stood in his doorway (which was securely locked and chained against the dark) and held his candle over his head and peered out into the terrifying night. The dark seemed to him to be waiting for him, and he thought in abject misery, tears running down his ashen cheeks, "I deserve to be dead.

It's true." He thought of the giant's horrible poem, Moranda, Moranda, and so forth and he realized with a new shock that the gallant armies had been lost for—of all people—*him*. It was *his* worthless life they had saved. "Horrible!" he cried. "Oh horrible!" and suddenly, hardly knowing what he was doing, he threw down his candle and unlocked his door and charged out into the street to meet the doom he so richly deserved.

But nothing happened. He stood waiting, but there was not a sound, ominous or otherwise. It was chillier than he'd expected, and he thought of returning for his stocking cap and mittens, but that seemed petty, somehow ludicrous, so he went on waiting just as he was, shivering and wondering where all the dogs were. After a while he began moving tentatively down the street, hurrying through the darker places, slowing down when he came to the street lamps, heading toward the darkest part of town, where perhaps he might come across some cutthroats. He was wrong, however. He went all the way to the city limits, and he never saw a soul or heard a sound except, once, a kind of noise like a pot breaking, falling from a second-story window a block away.

"Hmm," said the tailor. He scratched his chin and looked down his long narrow nose and thought, "What now?"

29

He realized with a start that he really was chilly, half-freezing in fact, and no wonder, either, because snow was blowing and the wind was howling, and there were icicles hanging from every tree in the woods. "How stupid," he thought, "not to have brought my stocking cap and mittens!" But since it might be warmer deeper in the woods than out here so close to the open road, he decided to go wait in the heart of the woods till the storm subsided. He started down the path that led in deeper, and he walked on and on, absentmindedly going past lonely hermits' caves and huntsmen's shacks and quicksand bogs, all the while staring down his nose and thinking he did not deserve to be alive, until all at once he came by accident to a huge castle. He looked up and realized it was the castle of the terrible giant. "Oh dear," he said.

No sooner had he spoken than a voice roared from a second-story window, high in the night, higher than the moon, "Ar *har!* What luck!" It was the giant.

The tailor instantly ducked into the woods, realizing in great alarm that perhaps he had reasoned wrong and did not deserve to die after all. "Perhaps the capture of the army was inevitable," he thought. "Besides, it's an occupational hazard of that occupation. If only I'd thought all this out in more detail, in the morning, say, when my mind was fresh!" His knees were knocking, and not from the cold.

Meanwhile the giant was shouting out the window to his dogs (which were enormous, larger than elephants, larger than houses, and every red tooth was seven and a half feet long) "Sic 'em!" The dogs came thundering into the forest, knocking down trees with their terrible shoulders, and their eyes were like lightning and their shaggy coats rattled and snapped with electric sparks in the cold wintry air.

"Heaven help me!" thought the tailor, but not so much from fear of the dogs as from his dreadful confusion. Did he deserve his fate or didn't he? That was the question. He sat huddled up under a frozen log turning the question this way and that way—guilty or not guilty?—thinking, "Blast! If I'd just brought my mittens!"

The dogs all ran past him, never noticing, and soon they came to some quicksand, and down they sank.

Then the giant was angrier than ever, and he yelled down from his upstairs window, "Where are my cutthroat boys? Cutthroats! Get out there and find me that tailor!"

No sooner had he spoken than sixteen huge boys came running from the kitchen with knives and cooking forks, howling like wild men, licking their lips and spraying salt in the air, and their teeth glinted like yellow pearls, and sparks flew out like shooting stars when they ground their teeth together.

charles shields

But the tailor hardly noticed. "I was a coward," he was thinking. "But is cowardice a crime, officially? I wonder how the Law reads." He pounded the sides of his head with his fists, but he couldn't remember what the Law said, exactly, assuming he'd ever known. And so he went on thinking and thinking and thinking, and the cutthroats rushed past him and away in the direction the dogs had taken, and soon they came to the quicksand, and down they went.

"Fools!" yelled the giant, and in his terrible rage he began to hurl flowerpots into the forest, hoping he might brain the tailor or, at very least, get him to show where he was. But the flowerpots fell to left and right of the tailor, who was lost in tortured thought, and didn't touch a hair of his head.

"Moranda," the giant howled at last, "get me my coat and stocking cap and mittens. It appears I'll have to go after that fellow myself."

Soon, sure enough, out came the giant in his coat and stocking cap and mittens, hunting for the tailor. The tailor absentmindedly watched him march past in the direction the dogs and cutthroats had taken, and absentmindedly watched him step into quicksand and sink out of sight, flailing his arms and yelling "Zounds!"

Then suddenly it all came clear in the tailor's mind. Before he could tell for sure whether he really deserved to die or not, he must see whether the giant had actually eaten the armies he'd carried off to his castle. So the tailor got up and walked resolutely into the castle and began to hunt around.

"Excuse me," he said to a huge old monstrously ugly woman he found in the parlor, "which way is it to the dungeon?"

"Third door on your left," the old woman said.

"Thank you," he said, and he went where she'd told him. There he found the king's two armies, bound up in heavy ropes. Quickly taking out his tailor's scissors, he cut them free, and they all fled the castle like water coming out of a pipe. "Are you people all all right?" inquired the tailor.

They said yes, thank you. The giant had said they weren't fat enough, which indeed was true. They were lean as rakes from the exercising they'd had to do in the army, and also, being young, they weren't any of them more than half-grown.

"Then I haven't done any real harm," thought the tailor, looking happily down his nose. Immediately he remembered the huge old monstrously ugly woman in the parlor, and he began to shake like a leaf.

"Don't worry about *her*," the armies said, perceiving his distress. "Now that we're out of the castle she won't stir an inch in our direction. She's a coward, really." They laughed and slapped each other's backs.

"She's afraid of everything—dogs, young cutthroats, flowerpots dropping from second-story windows! We're as safe as safe can be."

"Ha, ha ha!" cried the tailor joyfully. For it was true, he saw. There at the door stood the giantess, making terrible faces, longing to come in pursuit of them but too frightened to stir an inch.

And so in triumph the tailor and the king's armies marched home, the tailor speaking earnestly of the lesson he'd learned, how fear is all in the mind, really— though cutthroats are a serious business, of course, and there are, of course, some dogs that would as soon bite you as look at you, and flowerpots *do* sometimes fall into the street, endangering the casual passer-by. "Nevertheless," the tailor said, but then pursed his lips, for he'd happened to notice that the king's armies were hurrying from one street lamp to the next, glancing apprehensively in the direction of every unidentified shadow, listening as if with stopped hearts whenever they heard the whirr of something falling.

The king was so pleased with the tailor's work that he gave him his daughter's hand in marriage. They lived happily ever after in the royal palace, never leaving it for anything, not even to go get the mail.

THE MILLER'S MULE

A miller had a mule that had grown too old to turn the mill wheel, and the miller decided to shoot him. But the mule said, "Oh, master, do not shoot me! Spare my life and I'll make you a wealthy man."

"Hah," said the miller, "a likely story!" However, the miller was basically a kindly person, and so he decided to give the mule a chance. "Very well, I'll spare you a while," said the miller, "but you'd better be as good as your word."

"God bless you!" cried the mule, and he showed such gratitude that, in spite of himself, the miller felt touched. Nevertheless, the mule was actually a wicked and spiteful creature, and had a plan.

That afternoon the mule carried the miller to the royal palace, and on the way he said to the miller, "When we come to the royal palace, let me do the talking. You simply agree with every word I say."

The miller thought about it, full of doubts, but at last he decided to give it a try.

They came to the gates of the castle, and the mule

exclaimed to the guards there, "Quick! quick! Take me to His Majesty, for I've brought him a horrible traitor to the kingdom!" The miller was surprised at the mule's words, but when the guards looked at him inquiringly, the miller, remembering his agreement, nodded to the guards and told them, "It's just as the mule says." And so the mule and the miller were taken to the king.

When they reached the throne room, the mule fell down on his knees and said, "Your Majesty, I've brought you a horrible traitor to the kingdom. If I were you I'd chop off his miserable head."

"A traitor?" said the king. "You say this miller's a traitor?"

"He admits it himself," the mule said, and when the king glanced at the miller, the poor man, feeling uneasy, admitted it was so.

"It's a serious crime to be a traitor," the king said. "What has the miller done?"

The mule answered, "He claims he's mightier than you are, Your Majesty. He claims he can turn huge boulders into rubies."

"Well, well, well," said the king. "If he can, then I must say, he's telling the truth. I can't make boulders anything but boulders, try as I may. Let's see him do it." And he called his knights and told them to lead the miller to a field where there were boulders.

"Now see what you've done," the miller said in the mule's ear. "They'll chop off my head for sure."

But the wicked mule smiled slyly and said, "All may yet be well, master. All this is just as I planned it." And so the miller quieted his fears. He walked with the king's knights to the field where the huge boulders were, thinking the mule had some trick up his sleeve if not, indeed, some magic by which to turn stones into rubies. When they reached the field, the knights left the miller to do his work and went back to the castle. Then the miller turned to the mule for help, but to his surprise, the mule was nowhere in sight. "Ah ha," thought the miller, "so that's his game!" And he swore he would get his revenge. First, however, he would have to solve the problem of turning boulders into rubies.

For about a half an hour the miller walked up and down the field, dancing around the stones on one foot and shaking his hands at them and saying all the spells he'd ever heard of, but he soon realized he was no magician and had better try something else. He borrowed a shovel from an old woman who was sitting on a fence post, watching with one brown eye and one green one, and for the second half-hour he dug deep holes, hoping he would find rubies down inside them, the idea being that if he found rubies there he could dig up the rubies and put the boulders where the

charles shields

rubies had been and the rubies where the boulders were. But all he found was some bits of limestone and part of a ketchup bottle. Next he borrowed a hammer from the old woman sitting on the fence post, and he nailed up a sign which read, "Do Not Steal These Boulders," the idea being that when people saw the sign they would steal the boulders and he could tell the king, with an innocent expression, "I changed the boulders to rubies, but people came and stole them." It was a good idea, but the field of boulders was far from the road and nobody saw the sign. When all his schemes had failed, the miller sat down on one of the boulders and sighed. It was now almost sunset, and he knew that soon the king and all his knights would come and that would be the end of that. "What in heaven's name shall I do?" the miller said to himself.

The old woman on the fence post said, "About what, if I may ask?"

"Oh, these boulders," he said. "I have to turn them to rubies."

"That's easy," said the old woman. She waved her walking stick, and the boulders turned to rubies.

"Well I'll be darned," said the miller.

The king and all his knights came and saw what the miller had done. "You're a better man than I am," said the king, "and not a traitor after all." By way of reward, he gave the miller half the precious boulders.

The miller whispered in the mule's ear, "You spiteful creature, you tried to get my head chopped off. Now I will shoot you for sure."

But the mule said, "Didn't I say I'd make you rich, master? Do you think I didn't foresee exactly what would happen?"

"Hmmm," said the miller, and he didn't know what to think.

The mule said, "If you'll trust me further, I can make you richer yet."

"Hah," said the miller, "nothing doing!" However, on second thought he decided to try it. "All right," he said, "I'll trust you one more time."

That was exactly what the mule wanted, because he hated that miller more than words can tell, and he was determined to see him dead. "Oh, Your Majesty," the mule cried to the king, who was helping the knights load rubies into wagons, "I forgot to tell you one little thing. The miller claims that whenever he turns plain boulders into rubies, all the rivers in the kingdom begin to run backward, and soon the kingdom will dry up to mere desert and grits."

"What?" said the king.

The miller felt slightly uneasy, but he said, "It's true, Your Majesty."

The mule said, "If the rivers run backward, then the miller's a traitor to the kingdom, and if they don't run backward the miller's a liar. Either way, he deserves to lose his head." And the mule smiled.

"We'd better go look at the rivers," said the king. He ordered his knights to lock up the miller in a high tower overlooking the nearest of the rivers, and tomorrow morning, whichever way the thing turned out, they would come back and chop off his head. So they locked him up and sent the mule away and rode off to look at the rivers.

"Tricked," thought the miller irritably, and this time he swore he'd get revenge on that mule for sure. But then he thought, where there's a will there's a way, and he squeezed his head between his hands and tried to figure one out. He thought and thought, but the more he thought, the more he understood that whether the rivers ran backward or not, he was in for it. "There's only one solution," he said at last. "I'd better get out of here."

He set to work immediately. He borrowed a file from a hunchbacked old Friar with one brown eye and one green one, who was sitting just outside the tower door, and filed the iron bars from the windows. Then he borrowed a long rope and a lantern, and he began to climb down from the tower to make his escape. But he had forgotten one thing—directly under his window lay the river, and it rushed along at such terrific speed he could not possibly swim across it. "I'm ruined," said the miller.

Above his head the old hunchback looked out the window and asked, "Why?"

"Oh, because of this river," said the miller. "It's running so fast I'll drown the minute I set foot in it."

"That's easy," said the hunchback, "I'll just make the river run the other direction, so the water empties out, and you can walk across on dry land. Besides, some pirates are sailing away with the king's youngest daughter, and this is a good way to stop them." He waved his walking stick and the river emptied out, and the miller walked across on dry land. When he'd gone not more than a mile and a half down the highway on the other side, fleeing the kingdom, he noticed the pirate ship the hunchback had mentioned, and he went to it and rescued the princess and carried her back to her father, as was right. By this time the kingdom was beginning to shrivel up into desert and grits.

When the miller brought the princess to the king, the king said, "I'm very grateful to you. I don't mind telling you, son, we've been worried sick." By way of reward, he gave the miller half the kingdom and his daughter's hand in marriage.

"You're not angry about the river, then, or the kingdom shriveling up?" the miller said.

"River?" the king said. Then he remembered and shrugged. "All's well that ends well," he said.

Later, when he saw the mule, the miller said, "You vicious beast, you tried to get my head chopped off twice. I won't be fooled a third time—I'll shoot you now for sure." He drew his pistol and pressed the muzzle to the side of the mule's head.

But the mule said, "Didn't I say I'd make you rich, master? Do you think I didn't foresee exactly what would happen? Well, some people are forever suspicious and small-minded and devoid of trust. Go ahead, pull the trigger." Salt tears ran down his face.

"Hmm," said the miller, and he frowned in confusion and put the pistol in his coat pocket.

The mule said then, "If you trust me once more, I can make you the richest and most powerful man in the world."

"Hah!" said the miller, "do you think I'm an absolute idiot?" And he stalked away. But late that night he had a change of heart and went back to the mule and said, "All right, I'll trust you one last time, but you'd better watch your step."

The mule was overjoyed. "Good," he said. "Meet me at the palace in the morning." And so they parted.

That morning they met at the palace and the mule said at once to the king, "Your Majesty, now that you've given up half the kingdom to him, this miller has grown drunk with power. He claims he can overthrow all the kings from here to Latvia, including of course you."

"Is this true?" said the king sharply.

The miller was again uneasy, but again he nodded.

"Ha ha ha. He's kidding," the king said.

"It's no joke, Your Majesty," said the mule.

"No joke?" said the king.

The miller shook his head.

The king bit his lip. "And how does he intend to do it?"

The mule said, "He's invited all the kings in the world to come on a deer hunt to celebrate his wedding. While the other kings are hunting deer, the miller will be hunting kings. You'll be the first, of course." The mule smiled.

"What shall I do?" the king said.

"I'd chop off his head at once, if I were you," said the mule.

But the king said, "I can't do that. The invitations to the other kings have already gone out. We can't have royalty traipsing all that way for nothing."

The mule frowned, for that was something he hadn't anticipated.

"There's just one solution," the king said. "When the other kings come and the miller sets about murdering them, *I* shall go on a long trip, and perhaps when I come back he'll have changed his mind." He added, after a moment's silence, "It's a clever idea, that deer-hunt trick. I wish I'd thought of it years ago!"

And so it was settled. The day before the day of the

hunt the king set off to visit Yugoslavia, and the miller sat moaning and groaning in his room, thinking of all those kings he would have to kill. "Alas," he cried, half to himself and half to the princess who sat on the window ledge, combing her golden hair, "how can I possibly kill all those kings, even supposing I wanted to? What wouldn't I give to be merely a humble miller again, without this responsibility. Furthermore, they're my guests."

"Oh come now," said the princess. She was the most beautiful princess in the world, but she was mean. "No point in stewing over it. You've said you'll do it, so do it."

"But how?" cried the miller. He pointed down to the courtyard where the kings were assembled, each one with his thousand knights. "How can anyone possibly kill so many?"

"That's easy," said the princess. She pointed at them with her ivory comb, and instantly the ground opened up and swallowed them and then closed again, not leaving so much as a banner for evidence.

"You!" cried the miller, for only now had he noticed that one of her eyes was brown, the other green, so he hadn't saved her from the pirates at all, she'd merely been fooling around with him, possibly from boredom. The princess smiled. "All's fair in love and war," she said.

So the miller went on the deer hunt alone, and shot more deer than he had arrows, and came back that night and married the princess. When the king came back the miller told him he'd changed his mind, and so together they ruled the world from here to Latvia.

When the miller came across the mule, he said, "You traitor, three times you tried to kill me. Never again! Prepare to meet your Maker!" And he drew out his pistol and cocked it.

"Whatever you say, Your Majesty," the mule said. He rolled up his eyes as if to heaven. "But didn't I tell you, Your Majesty, that I'd make you the most powerful man in the world? Do you think I didn't foresee exactly what would happen?"

"Pah," said the miller. "The scales have fallen from my eyes, mule. You meant to kill me, and you would have, too, if the princess hadn't fallen in love with me, or perhaps felt bored to the point of despair, the princess being a witch for whom everything comes easy."

"Whatever you say," the mule said. "If you're sure you're right, go ahead and murder me. Heaven knows, I'm an old and defenseless beast, and in this world of constant uncertainty, it's your opinion against mine."

"Hmm," said the miller.

He held the pistol against the mule's head for a long time, and the princess sat in a nearby oak tree, smiling

and paring her nails. At last the miller threw down the pistol and stamped his foot. "Confound it," he said, "a person just can't tell."

He let the mule come live with him in the royal palace, since if it was true that the mule had meant to help him, it was only fair that he show a little gratitude. The mule never tried to kill the miller again, because if he killed the miller he would have to go back to living in a field, standing all day in the drizzling rain, like other mules. Thus as long as he lived, the miller never did make out what to think. As the years passed the mule became more and more friendly with him, and when the mule at last died he left everything he had to the miller, with a note so touching that the miller could not help but weep.

THE LAST PIECE OF LIGHT

Once, long, long ago, a strange thing began to happen—all the lights in the world began to grow dim. At first, no one especially noticed. People would casually observe, now and then, when they were trying to make out a definition in the dictionary, or trying to read the highway numbers on a complicated map, or understand the small print on an insurance policy, "Confound, it seems as if something's happening to the light, these days." But they were only half serious. They thought it was merely their eyes.

Soon, however, there was no getting around it. The world was gradually slipping into darkness. "The world's getting darker," people said experimentally. Shoemakers said it, and druggists who were trying to measure things—in fact everyone said it except the politicians, who furiously denied it—and the people were all vaguely frightened, wondering what it meant. Sometimes, in the pale gray afternoon, farmers waiting for their turn at the barbershop in town would say casually, but in a nervous voice, "I wonder if the corn will ripen before frost this year." The barber would shake his head and say nothing, for he'd heard it before, and it worried him, to tell the truth. None of the crops were growing right, and if this kept up . . . But it was not his business, actually, and neither was it the farmers' business, so they put it out of their minds, as well as they could, and talked politics.

The king called a meeting of all his politicians, and after he'd talked with them for a while about this and that, he said, as if it had just occurred to him and was not of much importance really, "By the way, gentlemen, does anyone happen to know if it's true, as people say, that something's been happening to the light?"

"Light, Your Majesty?" the politicians said, for they hated to come right out and confront a thing like that.

"Well," the king said, "I've been hearing rumors, from time to time . . ."

But they didn't pursue it. One was always hearing rumors, complaints, dire prophesies. What was a person to do?

Now in those days there lived a little chimney-girl, by the name of Chimorra. She hadn't a friend or relation in the world to direct or instruct her, and she lived with a cruel lady boardinghouse-keeper who gave her nothing to eat but old dry doughnuts and nothing to drink but stale tea. Nevertheless, Chimorra was a happy child, partly by nature and partly because, strange as it may seem, she loved her work cleaning chimneys. She would sit in the flue among the chimney swifts when everyone below had forgotten she was there, and she'd hum very softly to herself, rhythmically dusting the soot from the bricks, and she would listen to the voices in the house around her and think at every second word, "How interesting! I must try to remember that!" Sometimes she would remember and sometimes she wouldn't, for oftentimes it happens in this world that things which seem interesting in the dark are not very interesting or memorable after all in the common light of day.

Though she never went to school like other children and thus never learned the things her society considered important, like how to add nine and seventeen or what is the capital of Idaho, she did learn answers for a number of interesting questions. For instance, she learned why the best banks are in London, not Switzerland, and why there are no armadillos in the zoo at Minsk. Also, one day, sitting in the chimney of a withered old man with one glass eye, she learned what was happening to the light.

She overheard the old man saying to his one and only friend, who was a cruel old mizer who sometimes lived in Utrecht, "Soon I shall be Master of the World."

"Really?" said the mizer without much interest, for

nothing really interested him but money. "How so?"

"I'm stealing all the light," said the withered, one-eyed man and gave a horrible, horrible laugh. "When it's all gone, nothing will grow, and all the people will starve except me, since I am out of the habit of eating, and then I'll be Master of the World."

"Horrible!" said the mizer of Utrecht with a grim chuckle. It did not particularly bother him, because he never ate either, and he did not much care who was Master of the World, so long as they left him alone.

"My goodness!" little Chimorra said, her eyes wide in the darkness of the flue, "I must hurry and tell the king!" She waited till the two fell asleep from drinking, then hurried to the royal palace.

But when she came to the palace the guards told her to go home and wash up, they couldn't have soot all over the palace floor, so she went home to wash. Alas! the cruel boardinghouse lady would not give her a drop of water. "What shall I do?" cried little Chimorra. But what could she do? So she went to bed and soon fell fast asleep.

While she was sleeping she dreamed that a beautiful, plump lady in a ice-blue dress and a crown of starlight came to her bedside and said, "Chimorra."

"Yes'm?" Chimorra said.

"I want you to do me a favor, Chimorra," the lady said. "Go steal me a piece of light before the last of it is gone."

"Steal?" Chimorra said, sitting up in alarm.

"Borrow, I mean."

"In that case, all right," Chimorra said.

"Put it in your locket and keep it there," the lady said, "and if anyone asks you what you're up to, tell them you're working for the Lady of the North Star."

"Really?" Chimorra said. "Will they believe me?"

"Just do as I say, dear," the lady said, and Chimorra said she would.

"One more thing," the lady said, "and this you must be especially careful to remember, for the worst thing about darkness is, it's depressing. Also, what I am going to tell you is powerful magic, and there will come a time when it's needed. If ever you feel sad, just say to yourself—

> *Gloom is here, gloom is there,*
> *But I am the North Star's friend.*

After you say it you'll find you feel much, much better, because there I'll be—*ping!*—just like that! Can you remember?"

"I'll try," said Chimorra. To fix it firmly in her mind —and also because the lady did not look as if she completely trusted her—Chimorra said it over.

> *Gloom is here, gloom is there,*
> *But I am the North Star's friend.*

"Yes," she said then, nodding. "I think I've got it. It's

an interesting poem, actually. You think it's going to rhyme and then it doesn't."

"It's free verse," said the lady. Then she vanished. The next morning when Chimorra awakened she thought at once of the visitor who had come to her in the night, and some of what the lady had said Chimorra remembered, and some of it she did not. "I must steal—that is, borrow—a piece of light," Chimorra recalled. And, lest it slip her mind, she wrote herself a note. "Borrow light."

Then, clutching the note in her pocket Chimorra hurried to the one-eyed man's house and sneaked in through the cellar door. Above her head she heard the one-eyed man talking with his friend, the mizer of Utrecht. "Tonight is the night!" said the one-eyed man. "Tonight I bring in the last load, and in the morning when people wake up, Surprise! No morning!"

"Horrible," said the mizer, bored.

Then they sat drinking whiskey till they both fell asleep.

As soon as she heard their regular snoring, little Chimorra crept past the parlor where the two were sitting and went hunting through the house till she found where the one-eyed man had hidden the light he had stolen from the world. It was all in an enormous crock in the pantry, tucked out of sight behind crates of apples, sacks of potatoes, old catalogues from seed houses, and a giant pile of zucchini. Even before she

lifted the lid she knew she had found what she was after. The crock was humming inside as if filled with bees. She closed her eyes tight (since looking directly at that much light would be worse than looking at the sun), and lifting the lid of the crock quickly, she reached in and snatched a small sliver of light and hastily put it in her locket, as the lady had commanded. Then she fled back past the parlor and home to bed.

When Chimorra awakened the following morning, the whole world was as dark as a pit, and all the people were moaning and sighing, horribly depressed.

Chimorra said to the boardinghouse lady, "Excuse me, ma'am. Why is everybody moaning?"

"For grief, wretch," said the boardinghouse lady. "Shut up and eat your doughnuts."

Then Chimorra did a foolish thing. She said, "If the people are moaning because the light's all gone, then I am just the person to cheer them up. I have a piece of it right here in my locket."

"What?" shrieked the boardinghouse lady. "Show me! Show me!" and she grabbed a stick and began to swing it around in the darkness, trying to hit poor Chimorra on the head and steal her locket and get that piece of light.

"Stop!" cried Chimorra. "I'm working for the North

Star, and if you hit me I must report you." But the cruel woman went right on trying to hit her with the stick, banging away in all directions—if one can speak of directions in a world gone dark—and so Chimorra lept out the window and fled to the forest.

In the forest it was even darker than in the rest of the world, so dark, in fact, that Chimorra could not see so much as an inch in front of her nose. She groped sadly along past trees and tarns and wild animals' lairs and at last, quite lost and half-frozen from the cold, she crawled into a little cave and cried herself to sleep. When she woke up in the middle of the night (or so she imagined, for one could no longer tell night from day) she recalled, between sobs, that there was some sort of poem she was supposed to say when she felt very depressed, but try as she might she could not recall what it was. "Something stupid," she thought. "I remember it failed to rhyme." Then she said, "Well, stiff upper lip, I always say."

To her great surprise, a voice said, "That's a very brave thing to say. It's very moving."

"Who are you?" said Chimorra. "I'm working for the Lady of the North Star." But the voice said nothing, apparently no more impressed than the boardinghouse lady had been, which shows you exactly how terrible things were, so Chimorra said more timidly, "Who are you?"

"No one," said the voice. It came closer now, but she was not alarmed, for the voice seemed kindly. "That is to say, I'm no one any more. I used to be a prince, and I came out here hunting, but now in all this darkness I've lost my dogs and horses and things, and I don't know the way to the castle, so I'm no one."

"Unhappy man!" said Chimorra.

"It's kind of you to say so," said the voice. He began to sob.

Chimorra felt her way to where the prince was and patted his shoulder. "Buck up," she said. "I've worked inside chimneys all my life, and I'm not as bothered by the dark as most people. I'll guide you about. Perhaps sooner or later we'll discover the castle."

"You're very kind," the prince said, and he fell in love with her on the spot. When morning came they found it was still as dark as pitch, and the wind was colder than before.

Meanwhile, back in the village, the boardinghouse lady went on beating the walls of the kitchen with a stick, trying to hit Chimorra on the head, until finally the neighbors came over to find out what was wrong. The woman was by now so furious that they couldn't get a word of sense from her, and it was worth a man's life to get within sixteen feet of where she raged. A crowd gathered, hundreds of people. At last the king himself appeared, and he said, "What's all this commotion? This is your King speaking."

Presently the woman left off swinging her stick and collected her wits and curtsied, impressed at being visited by the king.

"Your Majesty," the boardinghouse lady said, "it's about my tenant Chimorra. I've learned that she's working for the North Star, and she's gotten hold of the last piece of light. I hoped to persuade her to give it to me, since I knew Your Majesty could find some use for it, what with all this dark."

"Hmm," said the king. "Very suggestive. A piece of light would be worth all the gold in the kingdom right now." He called for his guards and told them to hurry and make a search and bring him the girl. In no time at all the guards found the open window and knew she had fled to the woods.

But they were not the only ones who knew! For who should be standing at the king's left elbow, unseen in all that darkness, but the withered old man with one glass eye, and at *his* elbow his one and only friend, the wicked old mizer of Utrecht. The man with one eye wanted to find the girl to steal back his light so she couldn't foil his plot. And the mizer of Utrecht wanted to find her so he could trade off the piece of light for all the gold in the kingdom.

"Hssst!" said the one-eyed man, "we must get to her first."

charles shields

"Yes indeed," hissed the mizer of Utrecht, not mentioning his reasons.

The one-eyed man said, "Quick, I have a plan."

"You would," said the mizer.

They felt their way back to the one-eyed man's house and there the one-eyed man disguised himself as the Lady of the North Star. (It was dark and he didn't really need a disguise, but the one-eyed man was stupid.) "This ought to get her," the one-eyed man said. "Ha ha ha," laughed the mizer grimly, and loaded his revolver.

How dark it was, there in the heart of the woods! The owls who normally lorded the night on wings as silent as drifting snow were forced to walk on cold, hard ground for fear they might bump into oak trees and break their necks. And how cold it was! The bears went into hibernation, though it was summer, theoretically, and one couldn't walk six feet without snapping a snake that had turned to an icicle there on the path.

But the prince and Chimorra groped on through the darkness, farther and farther into the forest, foolishly imagining again and again that at the next turn they would come to the king's palace. Welaway! They were mistaken. They were coming to a terrible icy cliff that dropped away to the Atlantic Ocean, which was darker even than the heart of the forest, so that no one would see them if they floated there a hundred years, not even an eagle or a whale.

But four feet from the edge of the cliff, Chimorra stopped suddenly, listening, for she believed she'd heard a voice. And she had.

"Chimorra," the voice called softly and sweetly. "Come back! Don't you remember me, dear?"

"I can't say I do, really," said Chimorra. However, she did have a kind of suspicion. No one had ever called her "dear" but the Lady of the North Star.

And so Chimorra was half-inclined to believe the voice when it said a moment later, "Why this is your old friend the Lady of the North Star." Right after the words came a noise like wind or like a snake laughing, and Chimorra felt uneasy in her heart.

"I'll go with you," said the prince.

But Chimorra said, "No. Stay here. I'll go, and if I don't come back—remember me!" With that she kissed the prince on the cheek and pressed something cold into his hand—it was her precious locket—and she groped away into darkness toward the voice. The prince waited, listening with all his ears, but no sound came to him for hours. Then his father the king found him—he and a large group of cheerful politicians— and they all, by pure luck, found their way back home to the castle.

They lived on in the dark castle for many years, growing colder and weaker from hunger every hour. But cold and hunger were the least of it. The terrible part was the spiritual gloom. The king and queen wept all day and all night, and the guards wept in the courtyard. The politicians didn't weep, but they spent all the time arguing. As for the commoners, the bankers wept in their iron cages, and street sweepers leaned on their brooms and wept, and the laundrywomen howled as they hung out their clothes. Only the prince kept anything of his normal good spirits, for he remembered Chimorra's saying "We have nothing to fear but fear itself" (or something), and it gave him pluck.

Chimorra, meanwhile, had a sad life. For the voice was not that of the Lady of the North Star but the voice of the one-eyed man. He and the wicked mizer of Utrecht had seized her and had made their way back, by pure luck, to the one-eyed man's house, and since they couldn't find the locket, had made her their cook and cleaning woman, and year after year they worked her and tormented her and allowed her no comforts, not even so much as a pet.

But one night—the coldest night in the world—the mizer said crossly to the one-eyed man, "I'll tell you the truth. I'm sick to death of this cold and dark. A man can't *count* properly in this confounded gloom."

With the word *gloom* a light flashed on in Chimorra's mind, and she said to herself—

> *Gloom is here, gloom is there,*
> *But I am the North Star's friend.*

Instantly, she felt much, much better, and the mizer of Utrecht, in the very act of aiming his revolver at the one-eyed man's voice, began to squint and cover his face with his hands, and so did the one-eyed man, for something amazing had happened. The Lady of the North Star, who all this time had been chewing her lip and thinking, "*Think*, you little idiot!" was freed at last by those magic words and was able to act—and not a second too soon. Quicker than lightning she went to the prince and whispered crossly into his ear, "Open up the locket, stupid. What do you think she gave it to you for?" The prince opened the locket, feeling sheepish, and out burst the last piece of light in the world. It glanced off the mirror, growing larger there, and bounced off the jewels in the prince's crown, growing larger and larger, and it filled the chandelier and splayed over the waters of the castle moat and then all the village, and the people were saying, "Why look! Look!" And the world hummed with light like the noise of a billion cellos.

"Chimorra!" cried the prince, for she was standing in the window directly opposite the castle (his eyes had gone across to her straight as two arrows), and she looked exactly as he'd known she would.

"Your Highness!" cried Chimorra, but the prince couldn't hear her because of the singing and dancing in the street.

The prince hurriedly washed and put on his best clothes, whistling like a sparrow on a barn door, and soon he stood knocking at the door of the one-eyed man's house, and Chimorra let him in. The singing and dancing had stopped by now, because the people had gotten used to the light, and the village was not as pretty as they'd remembered it.

"It's so good of you to visit," said Chimorra, blushing wildly, when they were seated.

"How could I forget you, dear friend?" said the prince.

They both laughed merrily, then fell silent, then cleared their throats.

The one-eyed man and the mizer, standing behind the door, shook their heads, disgusted.

JOHN GARDNER, hailed by *The New York Times* as a "major contemporary American writer," is the author of such brilliant and powerful adult novels as *The Sunlight Dialogues, Nickel Mountain, Jason and Medeia*, and *The King's Indian*.

Born in Batavia, New York, Mr. Gardner grew up on a dairy farm. He has for a number of years taught Medieval literature and creative writing at various colleges and universities, and was most recently a visiting professor at Bennington College, Vermont.

Mr. Gardner lives with his wife and two children on a farm in Illinois.

CHARLES SHIELDS was born in Kansas in 1944 and grew up in Los Angeles. He has created paintings for record covers, posters, book jackets, and magazine articles. This is his first book for young readers.

Mr. Shields lives and works in Oakland, California.